The Wickedest

Also by Caleb Femi
Poor

The Wickedest

Caleb Femi

MCD FARRAR, STRAUS AND GIROUX / NEW YORK

MCD

Farrar, Straus and Giroux

120 Broadway, New York 10271

Grateful acknowledgment is made for permission to reprint the following material:

June Jordan, 'I.S. 55 Graduation Speech' © Christopher D. Meyer, 1969. Reprinted by permission
of the Frances Goldin Literary Agency.

Haruki Murakami, 1Q84, published by Vintage. Copyright © Haruki Murakami: Books 1 & 2 2009,
Book 3 2010. Reprinted by permission of The Random House Group Limited. Translation
copyright © 2011 Harukimurakami Archival Labyrinth. Reprinted by permissions of the
author.

'With a little bit of luck/We can make it through the night' from 'A Little Bit of Luck (Acappella)'
written by Joel Samuels (PRS) and Michael Anthony Rose (PRS). Published by GB Music
admin. Supreme Songs Ltd (PRS)/Mad Muzik (PRS). Used with permission. All Rights
Reserved. © 1999.

All photographs courtesy of the author.

Library of Congress Cataloging-in-Publication Data

Names: Femi, Caleb, author.

Title: The Wickedest / Caleb Femi.

Description: First American edition. | New York : MCD / Farrar, Straus and Giroux, 2025.

Identifiers: LCCN 2024017466 | ISBN 9780374616618 (paperback)

Subjects: LCGFT: Poetry.

Classification: LCC PR6106.E55 W53 2025 | DDC 821/.92—dc23/eng/20240422

LC record available at https://lccn.loc.gov/2024017466

Designed by Richard Marston

www.mcdbooks.com • www.fsgbooks.com

Follow us on social media at @mcdbooks and @fsgbooks

10   9   8   7   6   5   4   3   2   1

This is how we should begin to build another way,
another kind of humankind, a really new nation
— June Jordan

we cannot simply sit and stare at our wounds forever
— Haruki Murakami

amorawa o ta ba ri rawa
— Wande Coal

THE WICKEDEST

SOUTH
LONDON'S
LONGEST-
RUNNING
HOUSE PARTY
EVERY 3RD
FRIDAY
OF THE MONTH

(SECRET LOCATION)

the heart of a lit night

pulses

in our hands

DEFINITION

shoobs/shobeen/shubz/shobin

synonyms:

faaji, groove, bashment, house party, owambe

An institution for flight
not to be confused with an airport.
The oldest community project.
Think of it as a global summit or a conference on tax
[avoidance].
A swap-meet for delusions.

DEFINITION

shoobs/shobeen/shubz/shobin
synonyms:
country, homeland, nation, state

How does a country form? I play a song.
And you say: *oh shit this is my choon*. Another says:
ayy! rah! what you know about this! We sing,
half-making up the lyrics. Someone with
a pen behind their ear asks for paper.
A receipt is offered, the white space
is written on; a name and so a birth.
We, labour-room teary, spark lighters in
the air. Right hand over left breast. We sing.
National Anthem, our president says.
We sing to the flicks of her wrists.
Someone rips the curtains from the window,
shouts *FLAG!* We turn to it, salute and sing
a serenade to this baby country.

DEFINITION

shoobs/shobeen/shubz/shobin
synonyms:
dimensions, escape, weightless

the ting popped off last night
the DJ spun a tornado into the dance
& when we were in the eye of the music
the hand of God shook the room like a snow globe
& fifty-pound notes rained on us

Jevon Catches the Fever

don't call me   by my government name   not when I look this good
crime-scene stunning   commanding   your gaze   tonight
don't call me   what began   as a dreamwhisper   a name   flung
across the room   heard only by   my mother   in the eye   of childbirth

call me   that guy   the sponsor   moshpit organiser   conductor
of the shoobs   leng man   the skeng man   drippy drip lord
call me longgggg   distance stulla   silence eater   omo ologo
mister rise it whateva the price is   don gorgon   the champagne campaign of it all

call me by the name   my exes gave to me   in love   and in turmoil
silver   chandelier   *Mercutio*   swinging   the pendulum of my wave
tonight I'll be   tsunami   there is an aqueous ancestor   somewhere in my blood
call me   Bermuda Triangle   True North   magma under ocean floor

I could take   your woman   I'm sorry I really could
but I am much too in love   with myself   tonight
I am   the Fever   there is a tempest under my feet

Pass the Aux

Rank your bad days
in order of blackened hearts,
the worst a shuddering spectacle.
I know they expected you to die
at the bottom of the rock,
friendless and doom-sick.
It's late June   the month has been greedy,
fat off your misery.

                    In your twenties, nothing can kill you
                        the caption of your Insta story.
                            Six man gully-posing,
                                internet faces on,
                            heads hanging out the window
                                like a dog's tongue,
                            picture screaming horses:
                                bullet speed,
                                tantrum wind.

We Invented the Red Carpet

Butterflies on the scent of a syrup banquet,
        we arrive.
        Amina Muaddi heels and B22s,
groundwaters breaching the night,
scattered beads on a bridal train.
Reader –
      don't you like us like this?

               Very much undead
      •   dragged through the gut
               of the day   ambergris

    yet we smell delightful

    entering this secret city of flair.
This front door, portal.

The light is pinstriped and scarce
but your eyes see everything:
particles in the air – colliding nebulas,
the sandcastle in the centre of the dance.
One yout tells you that every grain contains
the memory of a night:

> *the night Shan's cousin –*
> *whatshisname, the red-faced boy –*
> *first met the woman he later married*
> *cos she stole his car keys*
> *so he couldn't drive home drunk.*

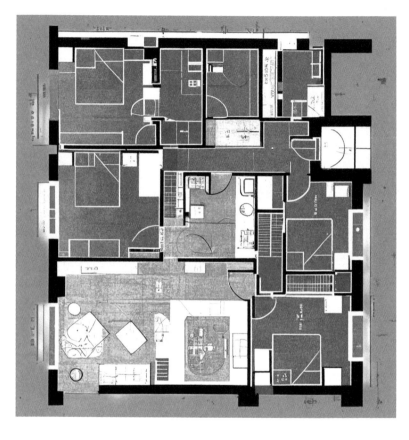

Fig. 1.3: *the wickedest [an X-ray]*

DJ's shout-outs

shout-out to the
gyal who step
correct,
miss goody
w'ya
rollercoaster

waistline

big up yourself   if you know   say   you're blessed
ladies   if you have a man   le'me hear you   tell him
                                                                mi!
                                                                ave!
                                                                fuck-you!
                                                                money!

remind him
your presence is a luxury

Lala

She saw herself more as a custodian of good times than a party organiser. For her, there was nothing to organise. It was already there: the people, the music, the yak, the vibe's spark plug and other ingredients that make a shoobs a shoobs. None had anything to do with her. And being that she was born in a La Bassine pool on that same dance floor, she too was just another ingredient, a cog in this community institution built by a man who now only existed in her blood.

It was rare that she danced. Most times she'd watch the people and their shadows: the leg-workers, the gossipers, stoosh gyal serving face, fingers rassing trumpets, lotioners, block bleeders, the wide-eyed outsiders lucky enough to get an invite. The crystal orbs of her eyes would scan the ebb and flow of community spirit. Her ears, blade-sharp, could hear the scorpion hiss of a Smartwhip which, of course, was banned at The Wickedest. Anyone caught with one would incur a one-year ban – her word final on it. And the people had no qualms because Lala was fair even when swinging the heavy axe of judgement.

Case in point. Lala once spotted Little Darren, squirrel of a yout, smooth-brained and still months shy from meeting the age requirement to get in. Yet, in he had managed to sneak and now hung on the periphery of the dance floor. Lala studied him: his eyebrows curved like a mathematician's, his muscles twitching, his Adam's apple gulping like a choking engine. Little Darren was there to catch his first whine. A canon event. Now, a custodian of good times needs tact, so Lala waited. Waited for the boy to find the courage to take a leap, and when he did – and knew for himself that he had the minerals to do so – Lala caught him mid-

jump

by the collar and
whisked him out into the night air.

On Est La Hein

Fredrick has an uncle who is staying in his room.
It was only meant to be a couple of nights.
Now it's been a month. Fredrick's house is
the type where an elder cannot sleep
on the floor when someone younger
sleeps in a bed.

In the morning at breakfast,
Fredrick puts in his AirPods
to drown out his uncle's sobs,
the acoustics of regret.

In the afternoon, as he irons
his parents' good clothes, he hears
his dad humming a complaint about
begging on behalf of a weak man,
hears his mum tune out his thick melody
with a fitting ayat.

In the night, Fredrick leaves the house heavy.
When he arrives at The Wickedest,
everybody knows him:
a drum roll of spuds,
Lala hugs him lighter.

The DJ plays 'Palazzo',
Fredrick beams, throws his hands up,
pries open the meaty air and tears it wide,
squeezing through into another dimension.

There, suspended in nothingness,
Fredrick is formless,
adrift in the deep,
yet to feel the electricity of brain matter,
yet to be choked by the asbestos of worry.

Fredrick Stick Talks in Another Dimension

if I say   I
came here one up
best believe I mean
I and I
that's II[1] man mobbing
real cool. drip flu. sneeze so
I can bless you
that is what I do now
send strangers my curated playlists
to prove anyone can be loved

listen
this is what I want for you,
a soft landing into the right arms –
isn't that what it feels like?
hearing a song for the first time
realising that it's always been playing
in the background of your life?
listen

I	*ain't folklore*	*fantasy*	*voodoo*
I	*can't grant you a wish*		
I	*am old-school like J Spades & as regular a yout*		
I	*will lie under oath but*		
I	*will never shame man for eating pum*		

---

[1] eleven, duh.

I   don't worry about what's on a next man's plate
I   have learnt to curb my intake of worry like I do salt
I   was just a stringy boy when I studied how worry morphed

        from
        nemesis
to
        pantomime villain
to
        imaginary friend
        who danced around my parents
        jumping on the couch where they sat
        a game of hot lava
        as they sunk further into the folds

Brenda dances with Jermaine

He loved to chew the seeds in oranges
wore leather   mostly.
He drank water,   made it look less ordinary.
From afar   he looked like he smelled good.
Up close,   better.

I've seen a rabbit caught in barbed wire
& learnt that all living things dance
edging closer to their void.

                                              my love
                          – no, he said   *babe, hold me*
                        so I know I am in something's path;
                    a boulder eating itself to become a cave,
                                              a home
                                              maybe

Corny shit sounds glorious
when you are spinning
in the arms of a mountain.
Deep in the part of me scalded
many times by betrayal,
I wanted to run – mace
the room & scream.

But he held my hips
& all I remember is

reverberating

gliding

like cherubs fleeing a riot.

Lala watches Jermaine (her ex) dancing with Brenda

Tentacles of a fire
drowning in the dark –
what beast is this man?

an unbridled
shame dispenser

I watch them sway.
His words

unit measurements
of disappointment,

licking her ear.

Long story short,
I loved a bushfire once.
He was a gold necklace sitting on
the collarbone of a dim horizon
& before I knew it
the doorknob was hot,
smoke had flesh, burning
through the walls
– the charcoal music.
We danced or
I wrestled a flame for oxygen.

Jermaine dances with Brenda

Could say we danced inside the soft guts of the stars.
Could say it was a lightbulb in a living room.
What I remember doesn't reside in the details.
It was a vibe in the shoobs – a proper oil spill.
Whole endz was there,
I arrived with Max & Jevon;
we came hot-stepping with lead feet.
Security at the door moved mad
we had to leave our bodies (& phones) at the door.
What a shame, my fresh trim woulda been a panty-soaker.
Still, we blew in like a blizzard.

You slow-whined with your girls
clutch bag in your clutches

litty committee
with the benz kitty

I slipped the DJ a twenty to play your song
& reload it three times.

this fucked country
my direct debits hit at midnight
the cost of living

I caught flashes   your smile or
                     your tears
What did you hear in the speakers?
Crows of a rooster? Dawn
betraying us like we
did our parents
sneaking away from our pillows
into the wet ears of the city

winter phantoms with no coats on
doused in Diesel
Magnums – poison to kill
anything in us pining
to matter to Babylon

Brenda, let me be of use
hold the sky up,   for you

myth says South London boys don't dance

Did you know that when a South yout is born
a leader of the community comes to the house?

That after the procedure is done
there'll be no more of him below the knees

& when he opens his eyes
he'll find a set of wings on his back.

So you see the other boys dancing
centaurs trotting

&
they say   *South youts don't dance*,

                  point up

                  to the murmuration.

**Neneng pulls an Irish goodbye and her Uber
driver tells her the lore of The Wickedest**

way before
people danced
they marched
thundered ground
shook pieces
of porcelain
from sky
marched morning
morning morning

someone's uncle
(Mig Jarret)
fell in
love with
someone's aunty
(Tippi Adan)
warmth shimmied
from his
chest to
his feet
turned march

to skip

a hop

etc. etc.

feet flexing
others saw
and laughed
said Mig's
a *dunce!*
Mig heard
dance! which
meant *more*
in mother's
tongue so
he marched
more more
as people
chanted *dunce*
dunce dunce

Mig danced
rumbled the
good seeds
out of
the soil
no harvest
brought famine
pangs panic

—   people called
Mig *wicked!*
but he
kept *duncing*
duncing dancing
until Mig
became a
kind of
people called
The Wickedest
people who
geese-flocked
to Mig's
house claiming
bomb-shelter
culture brought
them and
as they
all danced
the tonic
that perfumed
the wicked
room fed
the glutton
night until
the dawn
brought rain

they came like this for three generations
until the house passed down
to Mig's wicked granddaughter – Lala
who held tradition and kept her doors open
for those afflicted with the Wickedness

core memories [Max] I
after 'The First Time You Hold A Gun'

My mother's heartbeat,
the first time I heard a bassline.
Her womb, the first room I danced in.
How did it go again?
Kick cloud-soft twirl
stretch
black gulf
neon on my clay brain.
Kick . . . then
the drums fade
& her vocals come in.

[VERSE 1]

There will be strife,
burnt days, a god
— besides me —
sex & crueller colours
than the abyss
but there will be this.

core memories [Max] II

my primary-school disco, this girl from my class was dancing in front of me and for some reason felt the need to reach out and grab my shoulders, I panicked and grabbed her waist – maddest ting is, this girl had never said one word to me during our whole time at school, the whole thing lasted for about a second but the other kids saw and exploded into giggles, wouldn't let it go – urrgh you was dirty dancing, I'm telling . . . whining with . . .

I had forgotten her face until a decade and a half later, on a random night just last month, I saw her here . . . shocked at myself for remembering her but stuck . . . cos I couldn't just go up to her and say, 'yo I remember you from primary school' – could be seen as creepy or a lie to lotion her

so the end of the night came and me and my lot were about to cut when I felt a tap on my shoulder, turned around

we just stared at each other for a while then burst into laughter like two halves of a soul scattered across a field of lifetimes finding one another again

we laughed ourselves   headless
then we fixed up and went our separate ways

Abu the Wallflower Eavesdrops

Are you carrying soil in your Jacquemus handbag?
Heirloom seeds in the heel of your sneakers?
The entry fee is the first lie you told that set you free.

It's better to see this as an open casting
to play the role of main character.
A shoobs is a blockbuster movie.
The director doesn't shout cut,
he yells wheeeeel it up ta-bloodclart.

Epigenetics explains our rhythm
but our swagger is still a mystery.
The eye-rolls of the Black cheerleaders
in Bring It On *will tell you how that story goes.*

Almost ten years since his last attendance
and Big Tipper's aura is still here.
Close your eyes and feel it.

Sweet night air barren of fucks to give.
Baby, make your love visible
like the smudge of make-up on my shirt,
shadows in an abstract painting,
the dribble from your first bite of night fruit.

Brenda gives a pep talk to Abu

It is true what they say:
no drug is more potent than puberty
and after it peaks
the comedown
will last your lifetime.
One day you will wake up
to the fog already on your bed
spread like a lazy cat.
And in this haze –
this swooping ticking,
this scam that is adulthood –
you will become jaded,
washed of your colour.
Your juvenile eyes will harden.
The days will become sticky,
harder to rinse off your skin.
You will forget that your laugh
resembles the tongue
of a bell   whipping.
But you are not there yet,
tonight you are at The Wickedest,
in the left ventricle of the party,
unshackled and yet to be gut-punched.
So dance   with all the arrogance
of youffool stupidity
to the song rupturing the speakers,
the song spinning on the ceiling fan
over the room's bullish heat –
the outfit this party wears.

wicked she wicked [Benny's Ballad]

My skin is a rolled-up rug,
heave it onto your shoulder,
take everything I own.
Wild Wonder,
what can I do to be yours?
~~kill a thousand men~~
~~turn vapour into gold~~
I will walk with no gun
through my opp's block.
Torture me no more.

[chorus]
She wicked she wicked she wicked
Mi seh she wicked she wicked she wicked

The city's evening glow,
the dress you wore,
the third night of a heatwave – sleep
could not take root.
At this brink   we clung
and buckled through the fizzy black.
Love is to be full
in all that needs filling.

[chorus]
She wicked she wicked she wicked
Mi seh she wicked she wicked she wicked

You sound like a fire
truck when you laugh.
I used to have allergic reactions
to the sound of sirens.
I haven't yet had a rash
or twitch in the calf
or spasm in my index finger.
How frightening to think of tomorrow
without you.

[chorus]
She wicked she wicked she wicked
Mi seh she wicked she wicked she wicked

DJ's shout-outs

shout-out to the lovers in the house
big up the couple lipsing by the window
you lot been there all night though
you're blocking the breeze   please   kiss somewhere else

Boris Johnson came to the shoobs (uninvited)

During the pandemic, when public health restrictions
prohibited most gatherings, Prime Minister Boris Johnson
allegedly attended 17 parties.

Maybe he came here for cleansing,
to lower the cholesterol of grief,
feast on the ebullience of the mandem.

Maybe he needed to bruk out –
prove his good health or that rhythm, too,
succumbed to him like a loyal dog.

Maybe he came to present his neck
to our guillotine   wishes.

The question
of atonement exposes
a mark of gullibility.

Who was surprised
when it came out that
the man in charge of the country
was doing up guest-list whore
during the pandemic?

Not us,
not the people
who clean up when the parties are over.

Noise Disturbance

The wolves were pounding the door
but it barely flinched – made from centuries
of our skin – its hinges held
their nerve and the pool of saliva
under the wolves' wet jaws widened.

Inside, the air was loud,
the bass shook a mirage:

> my father, the DJ
> as he was before he became a holy man.

At the window – glassy canines peered in.
The smell of our lives was orgasmic
to them – the thought of locking off our dance
made their bodies throb.

> *I bet you they came in their pants*
> *police jizz like a moat around Lala's house*
> *lol*

For hours, they rammed the door
and when they stopped for breath
they snarled on megaphones that
our party disturbed the neighbours.

> *But the neighbours were at our party*

Embarrassed, they turned
their snarls into howls –
javelins piercing the cotton night.
Though from our side of the door
the howls were muffled by the DJ's   father's
voice, a weighted blanket
sending us love:

> *shout-out to the ravers inside*
> *who came to have a good time*
> *cos we don't always have a long time*

METROPOLITAN POLICE Working together for a safer London

PROMOTION EVENT RISK ASSESSMENT FORM 696

The use of this Form is voluntary. However, it is noted that the completion of this Form may be a licence condition on some premises licence. In that case the completion of this Form is mandatory in accordance with the premises operating licence.

Please complete this section to enable Clubs and Vice Unit to monitor the use of this Form.	
Is completing Form 696 for Promoted Events a condition on the premises license?	Yes ☐ No ☐
PLEASE NOTE - The use of this Form is not primarily intended for a live music event. If you are using this form for a live music event please give your reasons why in the box.	

Recommended guidance to music event organisers, management of licence premises or event promoter on when to complete Form 696 is where you hold an event that is -

- Promoted / advertised to the public at any time before the event, and
- predominantly features DJs or MCs performing to a recorded backing track, and
- runs anytime between the hours of 10pm and 4am, and
- is in a nightclub or a large public house.

The recommended guidance does not restrict the use of the Form solely to any specific event. Event managers and promoters may, if they wish, use it for events not strictly covered by the guidance. The Metropolitan Police Service will aim to give appropriate support and advice to ensure a safe event.

PLEASE COMPLETE ALL SECTIONS.

Name of Premises	*lala's yard*
Maximum Capacity of Premises	*unknown (it was built by the same architect as the TARDIS)*
Full Address	*round the corner from Munchi's*
Telephone Number	**Email Address**
Designated Premises Supervisor	*(redacted) see no. 828402*
Contact Telephone Numbers	

PROMOTER'S DETAILS	
Promoter's Full Name *(include any other names used)*	*lala Jarret*
Date of Birth (dd/mm/yyyy)	*fingers of light touched a plum half-chewed by a squirrel / autumn politely waited / a tree torn down as proof of my birth*
Address	*address me as Madam (if we are not kin) or simply L (if you've slept on my floor in the winter)*
Contact Telephone Numbers	Landline: T Mobile: T
Email Address	

PROMOTION/EVENT DETAILS			
Promotion/Event Name	*The Wickedest*		
Event Date (dd/mm/yyyy)	*Every last Thursday of the month*		
Start Time (HH:mm)		**Finishing Time (HH:mm)**	
Expected numbers attending event?		**Is this a regular event at this venue?**	Yes ☐ No ☐
Is the event... ? *(Check relevant box)*	Private ☐ Public ☐	**Will tickets be sold on the door?**	Yes ☐ No ☐

Please list below all DJ's, MC's, featured Artistes / other promoters performing

RESTRICTED WHEN COMPLETE

The police need the minimum of name and date of birth to cross-reference with their systems and data sources. An address is needed for confirmation of identifying the individual. It is recommended that the data submitted on the Form are verified by the person submitting this Form.

Real Name	Role and other name used (i.e. stage name)	Date of Birth (dd/mm/yyyy)	Address
Denroy Thompson	No blood		chases rum with water only / wears a string vest & oversize blazer year-round / hasn't had as much as a cold / went for blood tests once / three nurses tried to extract blood from his veins / not a drop was drawn out / they sent him home
Jerome Distry	pug		the name came from the fact his pupils are always dilated / says he sees the fine hairs of souls bouncing in the air / flickering
Maxe-way Diop	customs		born on the flight from Dakar to London / somewhere above the Atlas / mother had false documents / a nightmare / for customs at Heathrow as that same day the towers in New York were felled / as all planes were then grounded / they let mother & child into the country

Sonnet 696

What could go wrong if we so happen
to end up under the same roof; a party,
summer barbecue, will we all combust?
When I am in my room alone, midnight
lights off, Blackness makes sense as every thing
looks like me: a fork, bed frame, the rug, worn socks.
In blackness the room looks like a nightclub.
I look like a nightclub. Everywhere in
the city, in all nightclubs, the powder
of Blackness settles on everything. Truth
is that the mirror has never called me
haven but I recognise a fortress,
a room in blackness, twice cooked in shadows,
arms waving, making angels in Black dust.

Block-hugger, Knock-Down-Ginger Champion, Former Happy-Slap TV host, Mr buck-me-50p, the big-head idiot bulging on laughter in the acoustic section of the party, leaning on the kitchen island, surrounded by a foam of people, making a case for the Chimera Ant arc.

You, wearing your mother's smile,
flaunting it like a liver
on the black market.

my bruddas, I love you
with all the good
all the wild in me
what is suffering for
if not enjoyment
this could be our last dancing night
the day is dangerous
we know that

the bathroom mirror narrates Max's lineage
[Wishbone]

your mother | your father
a wishing well | a rusty coin
              sinking
is how they danced
              proof of love

          the purple of the night asks,
          what is the softest point in a wishbone?
          [your name]
          say it
          jump into flight
          you frail bird escaping
          out the ear of a snare trap
          you cunning
          wicked
          good
boy of a trillion
with molten iron in his belly
who lost his face
and the vigil in his chest
down the drain pipe of *IC3*
          this is how you survive
          water   thick air
          brick   boredom

          two-stepping
          at
          two o'clock

until new light
haemorrhages
through the walls

o hungry night
make me
or
obliterate me

destruction dance: a tutorial

cos i can't save my cousins
outside   fleeing by
sea   sand   mud

cos my bloodline
did not know the abundance
of sound until LimeWire

cos i've been eating sound
since ice-cream van melodies.
what is the

nah linga
azonto betha kick
gun lean?

the recording   of our history
spirit braille etched
into the tectonic plate beneath us

our souls are stronger
when our bodies
prove their conviction.

I wish I was naturally light-footed
but it takes lifetimes to learn
the dance of acceptance;
how to pivot around destruction
as I move through the days.

every shoobs is another shoobs

don't stand & serve
you are not wallpaper
even a stiff head nod
                    like a broken action figure
                                        at peak intervals
                                                    will do

could have been opps, bills, the weather or boydem,
in the sheath of your bed or
in the wilderness of the streets,
something tried to stop the motor of your heart
& something failed
every time
you survived the daily cull   again

take joy
spite's sharpest weapon   use it

                                    come here
                        ok, you will now be called we
                                now we are stronger
                                    now we laugh
                                        we sweat
                            we turn our bones to silk
                                we mock ourselves
                                for dodging arrows
                            while wearing blindfolds

a shoobs proves that
we are all afflicted
with Peter Pan syndrome
that we're all in the same gene pool of joy
a shoobs belongs
to a lineage of shoobs

> we walk suede
> metamorphose
> into our parents, uncles and aunties
> our Issey Miyakes stretch
> into butter-gold aso-okes

a mint November night
the dancefloor smoky like the jollof being served
the Fújì band speaking only to our waists

> we are a talking drum solo
> away from immortality
> sho ta leno
> o fine gaan

dollar bricks
ripped out of plastic wrapping
a shower of blessings
cash money falling
on our heads like a bounty

> if we are the wanted
> so be it

cash money falling
to the ground like a carpet of autumn leaves

we'll call that a win
for tonight at least

cash money falling
and the curse placed on the endz lifts

we dance with open ribcages
smiling in the face of Death
peeking at us from the shadows
our defiant hearts thumping
thumping
thumping

Famous Party Lies

- Fanfare and poppers welcome the first to arrive
- The last one to leave has nowhere else to go
- If it's lit on Instagram stories it'll be lit when you get there
- The more crimes in your bloodline the less natural rhythm in your body
- Forward, together
- For the many, not the few
- There ain't no party like an S Club party
- Link up soon
- [*putting your hands in the air like you don't just care*]

DJ's shout-outs

Mandem, I need you
to take it easy on the oud.
It's like a fumigation in here.
For the sake of our nose cavities,

relax!

Benny the House Regulator

Amapiano drum patterns
sound like yassified gunshots

Amapiano drum patterns sound like yassified gunshots.
What are we to learn from this?
If the pitch is correct,
what scares you   makes you groove.

I might fuck around,
cut loose the chain
anchoring me to the ground.

Have I told you about the pool
in my mind?
It's filled with oil wata,

contains versions of me like pickles in brine –
me at my kindest,
even when it nearly cost my life.

I dive in, the melody
the rippling vocals of a mermaid –
what are we to learn from this?

Dancing is your body falling from a skyscraper
and suddenly learning flight.
I want to be this sudden – I want to be

a moment crossfading over moments
like the DJ's mixing
as he calls out *piano piano*

and we scream back pianoooooo pianooooooo.
I know how to save a life – we all do –
it's what to do with it afterwards,

keep bracing for the next crisis?
LMAO –
fuck outta here with that.

Every morning the sun comes up
smug and unconcerned about my little life –
what are we to learn from this?

Humour will keep your abs in great shape
and make it easier to stomach
the terrors we are force-fed.

This fabric on my skin is expensive.
Only two specialists in the city
know how to dry clean it.

Come dance with me, baby,
it'll feel like your first time flying,
the glide   – frictionless.

I watch the last breaths of the night,
shallow and dignified;
I'm convinced I've met its cousin in Jo'burg.

The night asks me if it has been good to me —
I lie to be kind.
Tobi's laugh brushes past my shoulders,

I trace its path back
to a huddle of echoing bellies,
a meteor shower.

Where are we?

Marginalia

Full Capacity
a kitchen discourse on fitting in

Get in where you fit in
is a hood proverb
we've lived by since day dot.

> In academia, this known as
> the Clown Car Phenomenon.

I berate my parents for their hoarding obsession
as if I don't know how much they lost
just to fit in *here*.

> My generation are digital hoarders –
> hypocrisy is a well-fitting glove.

When I first came to this city as a boy
four languages lay snug in my throat
until I learnt that if I wanted to fit between
a rock and a pigeon-blood cloud,
there was only one language to scream in.

> How many meltdowns can you have
> before you realise the joke is on you?

Gen Z laugh at us
cos we wore business attire to the club,
attempting to fit the mould of a *worthy* reveller,
so many winter nights stood in queues
holding our bodies stiff,

                                    the cutting wind licking the shine off our faces,
                                          origins of the mannequin challenge.

I promised an orange moon
I'd never to fit into an imagination
other than mine.
I break it every time I tell my bruddas:
nah my G I'm tryna be like you
I'm tryna be fly
like you.

DJ's shout-outs

Juice your cup & hold a leng gyal
between your arms before
she finds someone who will.
Charm each other.
Tonight, you and her might fuck –
by the morning it might turn out to be love,
another reason for you
to keep on living.

02.59 a.m.

i

a party is always a bungalow
with multi-storey dreams in its foundation
anyone vibzing
has a claim to the deed

ii

the disk jockey is the keystone
a soundweaver
turning songs into
sonic Matryoshka dolls
(inside a song
is another song singing)

the 7 disc jockey principles

iii

what do we know of blacksmiths
samurais, surgeons, DJs?
the toil of their hands
the calluses
the popsicle nerves

iv

a murder could have occurred
on the dancefloor
when two opps locked eyes
one from Bush
the other from Grove
each not expecting to buck
a West London nemesis
in a south shoobs

all the while the DJ
had the dance jumping
no one else noticed the Mexican stand-off
each opp waiting for the other to blink
but before the spark of a bad decision ignited
the wave of the crowd
swallowed them

v

cos the music brings in
the boats that are not steered

vi

grit salt spilt over a frosty sheet
when they closed the last rink in the endz
we used wax as a substitute for the ice
the needle read its deep grooves
the speakers translated a treaty
& for the night
we would glide over a fleeting territory

vii

[a broken wing]
we are in your care
do not let us forget   flight

Max drops the [G] rave bop

I dance beside your grave,
trap mashing to the synths
of grass blades bending to the wind.

Of course with the little twist
I added to the bounce.

Your laugh still sits on my shoulders,
I have not shrugged since they took you.
The morning I found out
I ate cereal with cooking oil.

I suspect you already know that.

My G, what light is there brighter
than my sorrow? I know you see it.
Quit fucking about and come back to me.
I've got beef you need to back.
Lies I need you to tell for me.
Who's gonna gas me to whine with a sweetwun?

I am a dwindling river spilling
a current of bile and if only you
would let go of Death's roots,
your corpse will wash up
on the shores of your grave anew:
jaw, liver, spine, a filigree of nerves
attached to your buoyant soul.

Today is a good day for resurrection.
The whole endz is at Lala's shoobs.
Imagine the looks on their faces.
Us, crossing the threshold.
You, onyx-faced, dripped in white.
Me, your protector, shooing sticky hands away:

> *'llow it*
> *he just land road,*
> *touch him easy,*
> *touch him easy.*

either you
gully or gaza

        either you
        fate or dread

either you
fight or melt

        either you
        skank or sprite

either you
blink or glare

        either you
        walk or talk

either you
gasp or tut

        either you
        cut or burst

either you
gust or ghost

        either you
        sob or don't

either you
laugh or rot

                      either you
                      opp or gang

I said
either you

                      with us
                      or

you
not

DJ's shout-out

shout-out to the man dipped in butter:
I see you   big steppa   triple-stepping
the laser trim   dome like the Sistine Chapel
God bless your barber
                    for blessing you
                    for blessing us

ta na ne [Pris's Song]

Spaghetti language of my limbs,
I confess
my grammar is shaky
due to my sloppy two-step.
The sentences of my dance
have been the same since my teens –
year upon year
alone or palmed by friends.
I hope I am understood
when my body hears the song
and my limbs speak
what they have always spoken:

with a little bit of luck
we can make it through the night.

Shelly catches blindmouth
on the dance floor

a floating balloon
caught between turbine fans
that's how I got marooned
in the loop
of this melody
that's how I got blindmouth
and became a smooth pebble
at the gums of a lake
picked up by a toddler
who will show his mother
and say
pretty, I like this one,
it's pretty

God
until my final breath
let me remember this night

shoobz economics

the lengest of the leng / Pris and Shelly
cutting thru the crowd / turning the heads of dem
yutes from Woolwich / who rolled to the shoobs
in a six-car convoy / big ballers of the endz
the whole squad / had buss-down kettles
frozen wrists gleam / fucking disco balls

watch

how they call over Pris and Shelly / hood peacocking at its finest
jumping on the couch / *you do what you want when you're poppin'*
bottles tumbling / bowling pins
one yute / running game on Pris
another one / on the ear of Shelly

listen

if I asked you at this point / who had who in a vice
who needed to be on their guard / you'd say Pris and Shelly
but you're new here / just like these Woolwich yutes

look

again / not at the yutes
at Pris and Shelly / their slight hands
unhooking / the straps on the yutes' wrists
the blinding egos of men / slippin'
into their handbags

Max glances at Shelly

on the stairs
in the small shoulder of light
flickering in laughter
like a breaking storm

Decades from now
in the twilight of his life,
he will sit by a window
and in the distance
catch a glitch of lightning
and recall an echo of her face.

Fredrick shares wisdom with Brenda

mandem who fuck up and lose a good woman
don't cry and dance outside in the rain no more
these scoundrels are inside   dry
cosplaying the winner of the relationship
brazen animals draped
in a million-bucks sadness
silver teeth   subwoofer mouths
you'll hear them over the speakers   or if you don't
you'll feel them when they pass by
the air turning fuzzy
the voltage of heartbreak
spiking through their body

under a veil of sparked lighters,
Abu sheds a tear

Even when the music has me
glass-lunged and slimy with joy,
I think of you and spark my flint above
the canopy of hands.
The elegy ascends   my signal
that I once knew a marvel.

> *The first shoobs we went to*
> *they could smell the daylight on our skin –*
> *shell-toes, EVISU jeans, New Era caps,*
> *all in black like Narm youts should.*
> *Brittle like sales-rack hangers.*
> *Behind enemy lines in Blue Borough,*
> *we nearly died for nyash if it weren't for Lala.*

My gut tells me that you are here,
in the hemisphere of the party
where spirits dwell –
you've never been the type
to miss a lit shoobs.

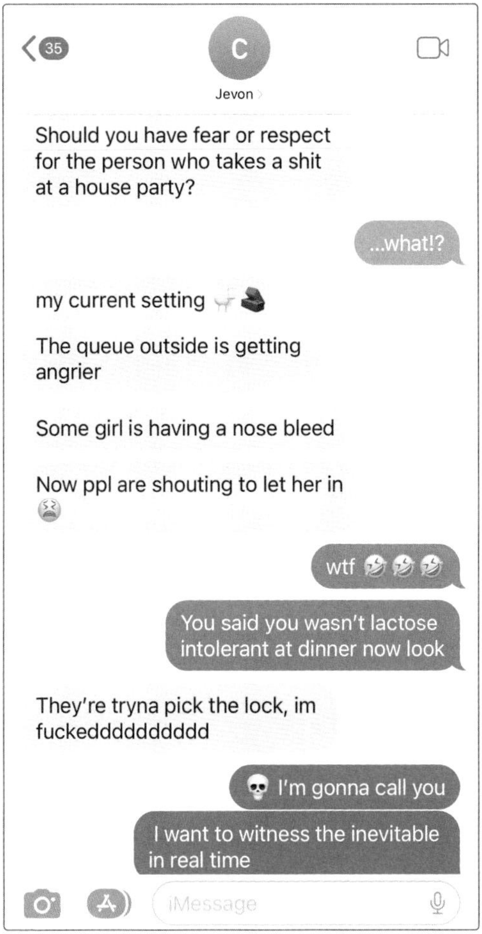
35
C
Jevon
Should you have fear or respect for the person who takes a shit at a house party?
...what!?
my current setting 🚽⚰️
The queue outside is getting angrier
Some girl is having a nose bleed
Now ppl are shouting to let her in 😫
wtf 🤣🤣🤣
You said you wasn't lactose intolerant at dinner now look
They're tryna pick the lock, im fuckedddddddddd
💀 I'm gonna call you
I want to witness the inevitable in real time
iMessage

27+

how cruel

creaking knees

how cruel

lower back

heavy buzz of youth

feet

cloud-dancing

the toll

rinse & cool

a shoobs never ends
it recedes

        &

washes back as does a wave
to the shores   we come to rinse away our failures

              &

cool our feet   the bunions
                  hot-road forged
                      the everlasting march
                      day in
                          day out

                              all good things come in waves:
                              unclaimed son of Max B
                                  his dress code was wavy
                          the wave brush in his side-bag
                    the black Versace shades
              the wavy gold head of Medusa
                  her finger waves hissing
                      a wave splashing the belly of the sun.

alone in a quiet corner, Benny opens the notes app

I check my list of defeats
when I forget how beautiful I am
are you tender enough
to un-monster me
time flies   my last shoot out
was fifteen years ago
the terrible face I once wore
look at me now   writing
poetry like a waistcoated griot
this romantic sleeve of life
this part of the dance
my favourite bit of the song (so far)
endless endless
depths of a laugh
swallow dark sky   whole
let me indulge
all of it

Max meets Shelly on the balcony

like a planet flung I danced
unroped fading into
the song's sublime colours

is this the seismic consequence
of looking the present in the eye?

I ran my fingers along the wall
the windowsill
feeling for the seams of the universe
an opening,   a glitch,
small tear in the cosmic curtain
to peel this papier-mâché reality.

I shifted through the hallway,
friends passed my torso
along the crowd's current
until I washed up onto the balcony.
More friends formed a choir,
sang at different pitches,
a breeze cupped a cool hand on my face.

I could have been a wicker crib
at the river mouth   drifting
oblivion

there was a woman leaning over the railing
the way a tree pokes
                    its fingertips into frothy clouds
she was on the phone speaking in Lingala –

money   *patience*   words I picked up
from when I used to trap in Camden
and found camouflage amid Francesca and her lot

truth be told, I forget how we got talking –
it gets like that at parties, right?
That moment sneaks up on you
when you and a stranger suddenly become
neighbouring fences –
a brief gust of wind –
she knew the epochs of my woes, my triumphs
and I knew hers

life is a pastiche
of other lives

it was the family
in the window of the block opposite starting fajr
that hushed our talk to silence

it's not a coincidence
that the music inside
the shoobs had stopped too

the balcony was the starboard of a yamal
arched shoulders
her elbows
            touched mine

the last two left
standing in a sealed pocket

and as the distant rumble
of the day's mad hum
hurtled towards us
there was enough stillness
to take the first
full breath of a new day

the only one we do nothing to earn

DJ's shout-outs

Shout-out to you,
who will outlive the rest of us
and carry the last memory of our youth.
The stubborn weight of our giggling skulls
painted in your years.
Remember us well.

And when you leave here, do not
speak of what you saw tonight.
If the outsiders ask,
tell them you saw nothing, no poetry
or anything worth calling [art],
only cobwebs,   stinky food
and trick mirrors.

[shoobs get locked, bagel king]

Acknowledgements

To my friends and family, you already know what it is – my love and gratitude is in perpetuity. To Rachel Mann – thank you for your support and guidance from the inception of this book to its completion. To nightlife architects Jojo Sonubi and Kazeem Kuteyi, all the rich discussions and musings we've had has been indispensable in the shaping of this book – thank you.

I am grateful to the following magazines and journals, where some of these photographs and poems have appeared, often in different forms: *Dazed*, *bath magg*, *The Poetry Review*, *Granta*, *Poem-a-Day*, *Callaloo*.

To Virgil Abloh, your legacy lives on.